TAD and DAD

By Stephen Mooser & Lin Oliver
Illustrated by Susan Day

WARNER
JUVENILE
BOOKS
A Warner Communications Company
New York

To Aaron Oliver, so glad you're my dad.
L.O.

Suggested for ages 3—7.

Warner Juvenile Books Edition
Copyright © 1988 by Stephen Mooser and Lin Oliver

Warner Books, Inc., 666 Fifth Avenue, New York, NY 10103
Ⓦ A Warner Communications Company
Printed in the United States of America
First Warner Juvenile Books Printing: April 1988
10 9 8 7 6 5 4 3 2 1

Library of Congress Cataloging-in-Publication Data

Mooser, Stephen.
  Tad and Dad.

    (Catch the reading bug)
    Summary: In this easy-to-read story, a young bear
comes to his father's rescue during two outdoor
adventures.
    [1. Fathers and sons—Fiction.   2. Bears—Fiction.
3. Stories in rhyme] I. Oliver, Lin. II. Day,
Susan, 1950-   ill. III. Title. IV. Series.
PZ8.3.05Tad   1988   [E]   87-40340
ISBN 1-55782-023-6

A Word to Parents from Bugs B. Smart

"Catch the Reading Bug" books use the *Word Attack* method of teaching reading. Word Attack is generally conceded to be the most effective way to teach reading.

What is Word Attack? It is simply a system in which sets of letters (such as *ad, ed, at*) are combined with initial consonants to form different words. To prepare your child to read this book, teach him or her the sounds of the initial letters, as well as the sounds of the set. Then, have your child combine the letter and the set until the sounds blend into one word.

In this book, *Tad and Dad*, the Word Attack set is *ad*. Teach your child how *ad* is pronounced. Then, when you come to each new *ad* word in the story, teach your child the initial letter sound and combine that sound with *ad*. With practice, your child will remember the sounds of each letter and be able to read all the *ad* words.

This book has two stories. All the words in the stories, with only three exceptions, are *ad* words. These exceptions are called *sight words*. The sight words in this book are: *and, a, the.* When you come to one of these words, simply pronounce it for your child and point out the letters that make up the word. By simple repetition, your child will come to recognize the sight words.

Set aside some time—ten minutes a day—in which to work with the "Reading Bug" books. If possible, stick to a regular schedule. Make sure that you and your child view reading together as a pleasurable activity. Point to each word as you read it. And, of course, be sure to praise your child's efforts. Positive reinforcement is crucial to his or her success. Go at your child's own pace. There's no reason to rush. After all, learning to read takes time and practice.

Reading and good books are special. If your children learn that simple lesson, you can be sure that, like me, Bugs B. Smart, they'll be hooked on books for life!

A Word to Kids from Bugs B. Smart

Hi! I'm Bugs B. Smart, and I'm a reading bug. I'm here to help you learn to read.

This book has two very funny stories. If you practice, after a while you will be able to read these stories by yourself. And that is a very grown-up thing to do!

Almost all the words in this story have the letters *ad* in them. Can you say *ad*? Can you read *ad*? Sure, you can! Let's try it. Point to these letters and say *ad*.

ad

That's great! You're a real reading bug!

Tad and Dad

Dad.

Dad had the pad.

Tad.

Sad Tad.

"The pad!"

"Tad! Tad! The pad!"

Tad had the pad.

Glad Dad!

Glad Tad!

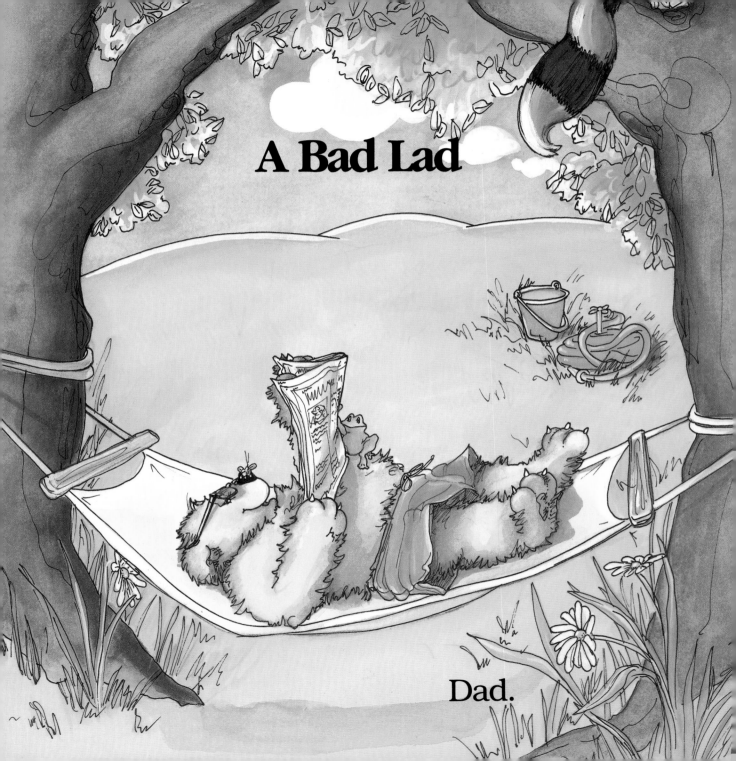

A Bad Lad

Dad.

Tad.

A lad.

A bad lad.

Sad Dad.

Mad Tad.

A sad, bad lad.

Tad and Dad.